Cover by Joe Fogle

IG: @cryptoteeology

28
Days
Sassier

For Bryce, Michael, and Riley.

The Bigfoot Boys.

Thanks for inspiring this.

I saw Bigfoot today.

Believe it or not, that's not the weirdest sight my eyes have had the pleasure of dining on in the past month or so.

If you're reading this, which Jim Tiptree(me) is going to doubt you are because that would mean someone came back to this dead dimension for some sort of scientific research. I really doubt a notebook in a third-floor hotel room in Columbus, Ohio is the place you're going to be looking for answers.

Here's the rundown just in case, then I can get on with the rest of my day.

Scientists are smart.

Smart scientists find a way to open portals.

Smart scientists didn't realize they accidentally gave a road map to the residents of another dimension.

Smart scientists say "ah, shit!" when these weird little green guys start attacking people like hordes of crazed chimpanzees.

The town of Hopkinsville, Kentucky says "told you so!" when the world realizes the invaders are the same creatures that attacked a small Hopkinsville farm back in 1967.

Smart scientists are all, "damn, they must be pissed about whatever happened back then."

Dumb scientists claim the original attack by twelve to fifteen of these goblins may have been a misunderstood diplomatic mission.

Dumb scientists get ripped to shreds on live TV causing smart scientists to try to get us all the Hell out of here and to what they call "Earth-2." A place where man has never existed, so it's like a completely fresh landscape for us to fuck up.

Portal centers open up in town, I go through with my wife, Claire, she fades from my vision, and BLAMMO, here I am stuck in the same place but everyone else is gone. Just in the middle of an empty building nearly blinded by the flash that was supposed to take us. Worked for everyone else except me.

Shoulder shrug emoji.

I don't know what happened, but something fucked up and I didn't get to go with literally everyone else on Earth.

Goblins take over and raid buildings at night for anything they can eat, which actually turns out to be concrete.

Goblins now live in the woods outside of the city I'm stuck in.

A city that is now an all you can eat buffet for them.

I gave up trying to make the portal thing work after a few days. It looked like a smaller version of Stargate hanging from the ceiling. They set it up in Newport Music Hall and turned it on like a massive flashlight.

Long story short, the first few days I spent trying to get the thing to work again; it wouldn't.

I tried to get a generator to work at Wendy's so I could cook something; I couldn't

Now I sleep in this empty hotel and leave every day to go find canned food and chocolate bars.

The other day I ate two whole boxes of Oreos for dinner.

That's what you would call a good day.

That's all out of the way now, for you, mysterious reader.

Back to Bigfoot.

I was sitting on a bench, eating a Snickers, when one of those little green fuckers flew over my head like it was shot out of a cannon. I saw a shadow, heard it shrieking as it flew over me, and watched as it splatted against the building across the street.

Me, being a genius, I deduced that the goblins couldn't fly because they didn't have wings, and I honestly hadn't seen them do it yet. Considering the amount of torture they've thrown at me over the past two months, I think that's something they would have used by now.

Also, if that's how they flew, all floppy limbs and ass over tea kettle until accidentally exploding against a wall, they needed to take some training courses.

I stood up and spun around to see what type of catapult device these things had invented to fuck with me. Turns out it was about nine feet tall, covered in brown fur, muscles, and a pissed off demeanor. It looked at me and showed its teeth, which were more human than monster; which when I look back on that I'm curious why it was so scary. It may have been trying to smile.

I didn't stick around to find out though. I said, "holy shit!" and ran back here to the safety of hotel bedding.

I calmed down after an hour of looking out the peephole and windows to make sure it hadn't followed me home like some weird new door dash employee; then I sat down and wrote this on a hotel notepad.

Tomorrow though, tomorrow I'm going to go back to that bench and see what happens.

No signs of Bigfoot, Sasquatch, the Yeti, or The Florida Skunk Ape today. I can't say I'm surprised. As long as I've been here, I only saw him yesterday, so he must be hiding.

I did, however, notice someone spray painted "Hail Satin" on a brick wall. They must have done it before everyone left, and I'm just now noticing it.

I spent all day thinking about it.

I had a jar of pears I found in an apartment, my little plastic fork, a Gatorade, and a bag of beef jerky. I didn't find a portable DVD player there either. I've been searching for one of those for days. If I could get back to my house in Athens, I wouldn't have to worry about it. But that's a long walk, and these goblins are faster than fuck boi.

The Bigfoot in that one commercial used to always get royally pissed off about people eating his jerky so I thought maybe

THAT was why he tossed that goblin like it was an egg and the concrete wall was his mean old neighbors' car. Maybe the goblin stole his jerky? That was my hope when I took the jerky; maybe I could offer him some and have a BFF.

I got in a ton of trouble in ninth grade for doing exactly that. The egg thing, not befriending Bigfoot. Or would it be eggsactly?

I've been here a while, ok? Cut me a fucking break.

Mr. Young, my childhood friend Devon's neighbor, he had this sweet ass driveway that was basically two inclines with a flat spot in the middle. My friends and I used to fly down that thing on our bikes and see if we could ramp the second incline from the flat spot. We were never successful, so I guess he didn't see any harm in the neighborhood kids riding down his driveway and telling each other how close we got. All the way up until Billy brought a little plastic ramp his older brother used for skateboarding.

Billy took off down that first incline going as fast as we all did but knowing there was an honest to God ramp waiting for him, he seemed like he was going faster than the speed of light.

I have a theory that the only way time travel would be possible is if you could move faster than the speed of light. You have to reach a spot before even sound or sight do, then you can travel back along the waves like the Silver Surfer.

Is that what he did?

I was never really big into Marvel, more of a DC kind of guy.

I wonder what Washington DC is like now? I have a hunch that the goblins have already eaten the White House.

May God show them kindness for that one favor they have done for the human race.

Billy probably wished he was a time traveler in Washington DC with a silver surfboard that day instead of the fifteen-year-old kid who was flying through the air with a bicycle below him.

He landed with his front wheel turned and flipped face first onto the concrete; I think people call what he did the scorpion? I don't know if that's an ok thing to say or not, but I don't think anyone is reading over my shoulder and Twitter isn't really running anymore anyway.

So, Mr. Young came hauling ass out of the door and kicked the ramp. His big ass work boot went right through the side of it, and he absolutely decimated the thing trying to shake it off his leg while yelling at us to not do that again because of something about his insurance deductible.

Yadda yadda yadda, Billy not only lost two teeth from the fall, but then his older brother kicked the shit and three bucks out of him for getting his ramp destroyed.

We went that weekend and egged that sucker's El Camino.

We weren't scientists, so little did we know about this whole "Angle of Trajectory" thing that Mr. Young kept saying to us when he was explaining how he knew the eggs were thrown from Devon's porch.

Our parents agreed it would be ok if the three of us cleared off a hillside on the other side of Mr. Young's house. Which it was, until we all got into a fight because Devon blamed Billy for the whole thing over the ramp, Billy blamed Devon for having a mom who cooked eggs every morning, and they both blamed me for not having the sense to say "hey, guys, maybe NOT the El Camino?"

The three of us tussled around and ended up just rolling down the hill, then we all cried and said sorry.

Billy became a Jehovah's Witness and Devon was still living in his childhood bedroom doing shrooms and looking at black light posters the last time I heard from them.

Let's talk about this "Hail Satin" thing a little more before I let whoever you are go.

What the fuck?

Did they mean Satan?

Or was someone out here worshipping a fabric?

The churches are fashion model runways. Wait, lemme try that again.

Runways are their churches and Calvin Klein is their God.

If Calvin Klein isn't a popular brand, I'm sorry, just pretend I said Gucci.

There's something there about how we as a society blindly follow these leaders who we know so little about. What's the difference between someone worshipping Satan and not knowing how to spell his name, and the people who follow politicians without knowing what the last movie they rented from a Blockbuster was before they closed down?

I couldn't bear the thought of voting for someone whose last great video rental choice was The Sisterhood of the Traveling Pants.

Never seen the movie, don't know if I used the right bear up there.

That rhymes.

What if they were satin pants, though?

I'm bored.

Hail Satin and try again tomorrow.

Bigfoot is not playing games anymore.

Quite frankly, I think he's pissed off.

Today I went back to the bench; which by the way, NEVER eat random peaches you find sealed in a Mason jar. Looking over what I wrote yesterday, and how I was up ralphing at 3am—THE WITCHING HOUR— I think those things were soaked in something.

I was kind of walking around the spot where the goblin hit the wall, I noticed there was a weird stain that looked like oil in a water puddle. Only it was a mix of Orange, Pink, and Blue, so they must bleed weird?

If it bleeds, I can kill it.

Shout out Arnold, what's up.

The chunks of concrete from the building were gone, absolutely no surprise there, those goblins probably had a late-night feast.

When I thought about that, my stomach started to grumble. I tried to tell it that if it hadn't upheaved all the food that I gave it yesterday it wouldn't be in so much pain, but nooooooo, lil' tum tum did not want to hear about that.

I turned around to go find some sort of sustenance, and Predator was standing there.

I swear on my dead ass grandma's crumbling gravestone and her collection of Longenberger baskets.

I took a step back, trying to keep my skull attached to my body and covered in skin; only to stand in the weird liquid the goblin left. My foot came out from under me, and I hit the ground hard. I was winded. I felt like I got hit in the chest by two thousand pounds compressed into a basketball.

Predator stepped toward me-

Let me clarify, I'm talking when he was see-through in the movies. When he was just sort of blurry.

Want some candy?

No, I sure don't.

It reached out to me with what I thought was its hand, I screamed and crawled backwards. In doing so I kicked some of the water-blood-grossness up on it, it jumped back and let out the loudest, deepest howl I've ever heard.

It made my bones hurt.

Where was Amber Midthunder or Danny Glover, the only two people who ever killed a predator.

I know if anyone is reading this they're saying, "WhAt AbOuT aRnOlD?" Well, he did not kill Predator. Predator used that self-destruct thingy. Also, he cheated! Predator wanted hand to hand combat and Arny made all of those traps. That's also why Adrien Brody isn't getting credit… not because I forgot about him and I'm too lazy to go back and edit what I said, but also too stubborn to admit I was wrong. Besides, Arnold already got a shoutout.

It slowly changed from Predator into Bigfoot, and I actually felt a little relieved, until I realized somehow Bigfoot was able to become invisible.

It looked at me and brushed the substance from its fur. The weirdest thing, as it brushed it, I noticed the spot would go all Predator cloaking device and then back to normal.

I didn't have a chance to process the thought I have now about that because I said, "I'm sorry, big guy," and he charged at me screaming.

He picked me up and ran into the doorway of a building, I felt myself floating up into the air before crashing onto the ground of the second floor. I rolled over and looked down through the hole in the floor in time to see Bigfoot had gone full Predator again just as five goblins walked in.

Little green fuckers must have seen us come in here.

I hate-stared at their green little heads, with their pointy ears. I thought to myself I didn't know you could pile shit three foot high, put shark teeth in its mouth, and teach it to eat concrete, but here we are. Not me hiding from them and thinking up jokes a pissed-off old man would make.

Bigfoot moved behind them and brought his fists down hard on the top of two of their heads. They smashed into the ground and exploded like gushers as their box of crayon blood sprayed all over the wall.

The other three turned and shrieked, they leapt at Bigfoot. Only one made it to him, the other two were grabbed midair in his massive hands and smashed together like a hamburger patty.

The one survivor climbed Bigfoot like he was squirrel and Bigfoot was the largest tree in existence. It bit down onto Bigfoot's head and then jumped off his back. Bigfoot touched the wound and pulled away a red hand.

Let me pause mid action scene and ask this question.

What the hell was my life even?

Why was I hiding in a building watching Bigfoot fight a Hopkinsville Goblin?

Paging Mothman, you're the next entrant in the Cryptid Royal Rumble.

Back to it.

The goblin moved quickly and slashed the back of Bigfoot's leg. Bigfoot went down on one knee and howled. The goblin covered its ears for a second and then showed its rows of teeth.

I swear to you, their faces are nothing but softball sized black eyes and rows of teeth.

It lunged forward with its claws stretching out of its hands and feet, looking like some deranged green cat.

I had to help, so I dropped down just in time to collide with it and send it off course.

When I stood up, it was looking at me with pure malice.

I breathed deep and said, "go on! GET!" like it was a stray dog rummaging through a trashcan.

The goblin dropped one arm to its side and flicked its claws out like the villain in some superhero movie.

All I could say was, "ah, fuck," and back up. As it paced toward me, I noticed this one had stripes all over it. It looked like a tiger or zebra; the stripes were just slightly darker than the rest of its body.

It hissed at me, again like a cat, and arched forward. I could feel it's spittle flying against my face, and I realized this three-foot-tall green asshole was genuinely the scariest thing I have ever seen, and I was about to legitimately shit my pants.

Then I tripped over Bigfoot's knee.

He looked at me and let out a roar, I swear if I could speak Bigfoot, I would have been getting called every name in the book.

The goblin took the opportunity and dove back on Bigfoot's back.

It dug its back claws in and pulled its hand back to swipe the life right out of Bigfoot's body. Only Bigfoot wasn't an idiot, he leaned forward and sent the goblin flying over his back by using its own momentum.

It landed and slid a few feet across the floor before getting its feet back under it and facing Bigfoot.

It hissed and showed all of its claws and teeth. I did think I was going to at the very least piss myself on this one, it was a little green human form with a million knives basically.

Bigfoot howled and stood up. Limping a little on its bad leg.

I tried to step in front of him to help and he shoved me so hard I hit a wall and fell over.

The little green fuck let out what I can only call a chuckle.

Evil little shit.

Bigfoot took a step forward on his bad leg and groaned, I could see the calve was cut deep and blood was flowing.

The goblin saw it too, it looked right at the leg, smiled, then let out another one of those horrendous laughs before taking off running deeper into the building away from us.

I heard glass shatter distantly.

When I turned to Bigfoot, I saw the flat of his hand for a split second before he paint brushed me into unconsciousness.

I woke up in the dark with a headache.

The sun was setting, so I had to move.

I looked at a cardboard cutout of a woman in an American flag bikini holding a twelve pack of Pabst. I nodded at her and said, "babes, bikinis, beer, Bigfoot."

Something WILD happened today.

I didn't go back to that bench. No way am I ever looking at that thing again.

Too much trauma.

Thinking about that bench gives me the chills.

Predator-Bigfoot.

Launched out of a canon Goblin.

Goblin with knives all over its body.

Me, an intellectual, deciding I'm better off not fucking with any of that ever again.

I went the opposite way down High St. today. I found a little shop I hadn't scavenged yet; good haul, lots of candy and chips. I did get a can of Wolf brand chili to try and eat only I didn't have a can opener and I really didn't like taking stuff home. The trash starts to smell like a bloated whale carcass filled with rotten tuna and milk in the July sun.

I tossed it over my shoulder and groaned in annoyance; you know, because I couldn't just eat it tomorrow or take the trash somewhere else.

Again, me being an intellectual.

I heard the sound of metal being torn and jumped off the curb I was sitting on. I turned to see Bigfoot fading into view again and said, "please, my brother in Christ, I am begging you, stop with the invisibility cheat code."

Bigfoot was still limping as he brought the can over to me. I reached out and took it; he had opened it for me.

I said, "wow, thanks big guy, I'll dance at your wedding," I didn't know what else to say and if anyone does know what to say to Bigfoot when he opens a can of chili for you, please let me know.

He limped past me and into the street. When he got there, he looked over his shoulder and grunted at me. He pointed down to his calve where the goblin had sliced through the skin.

It didn't look good at all; this cut was deep. It looked like it had started to clot into his fur.

I said as calm as I could, "let me try and see if I can pull the hair away, maybe we can clean it and seal it up."

I didn't even get to explain to him how my wife, who is a complete bad ass thanks to her weird survivalist parents, taught me how to make stitches with floss or any other shit I could find. As soon as I touched the hair on his leg he kicked out and shrieked. He accidentally hit me in the chest with the heel of his foot and sent me backwards on my ass.

I sat up just in time to see a few garbage cans getting split apart by an invisible force as he cloaked himself and ran as fast as he could away from me.

It's night here now. I finished my meal and came back to see what supplies I could find to maybe fix him up.

A little while ago I heard a door on my floor open and close. When I went to look, I couldn't see any signs of who did it; except for the trail of blood leading into the room across the hall.

Either Bigfoot was following me, or this place was haunted AF.

I need a nap in a bad way.

I had been woken up at 3:17 am.

The witching hour again!

A ghost pulled away my blanket fortress; the one I spent an hour building around myself so that I fit deep within.

Not a ghost, but Bigfoot cosplaying as the Predator again.

I put my hands up, begging him not to kill me.

He turned around and pointed at the cut again.

I'll spare the details, but it's sewn up now. He only kicked me once, after that I said, "hey, it's ok, I'm going to help you."

His skin was so thick I didn't think it would be possible. I had to push the needle like it was going into… something.

Something else that I found really interesting, when I would jam the needle into his skin, the area around the wound would go all Predator. It was like he could manipulate his hair into changing colors or becoming transparent.

Does Bigfoot share some genes with chameleons?

What I realized is that he's doing it when I hurt him; he's using it as a self-defense mechanism.

I started thinking about that while I was working. Does this mean that his species could possibly be all around us at all times? Are they silently watching and judging us as a threat or a friend? What would make a creature this powerful so afraid of humanity as a whole that they had to hide like this?

I started down a rabbit hole in my own mind. All of the sightings, all of the footage; could those have been test runs?

Picture it, Sasquatch as a species, they allow us a glimpse of their existence as a test. They want to see how we would react; would we treat them as peers? Pets? Food? Zoo exhibits? Or would we capture them and run them through painful scientific tests?

Given our track record, who could be sure?

I can't even say that I wouldn't have exploited capturing one for my own monetary gain; and I think they know that's how we all are.

Babes, bikinis, beer, Bigfoot, and CAPITALISM.

We would have exploited them.

I am confident in that.

As I sat there wondering about how he made his hair do that, all I could picture was soldiers covered in their pelts. Factories with Sasquatch being skinned and sold to the military for some sort of advanced warfare.

I can see an army of Sasquatch forced to fight wars in the same ways the poor are.

What would they use to manipulate Bigfoot though? With the poor and underprivileged it's money and college.

But what if it was Bigfoot?

I had a feeling it could be as dark as children kept in cages, being held hostage.

Families of these creatures being separated and sent to fight human wars for inhuman leaders.

What would happen to the children when the parent didn't return? Would they be left in the cage to grow old and then be trained to take their mother or father's place?

Maybe my imagination is getting the better of me here, but I did just sew up a laceration on Bigfoot's calve. Not really what you'd call an everyday thing.

I watched as he started to fall asleep, he started the transition into Predator cloaking.

He turned and looked at me, then the cloaking dropped. He was laying there in full view, snoring away. Maybe we could be fixed as a species.

*

I slept on the couch in the room after writing all of that. I was woken up by the door closing. I looked out the window and saw him leave the front of the hotel and fade into invisibility. I decided I'd stay home today; this was all getting to be a bit overwhelming. I sat around sleeping on and off for most of the day.

When I woke up around 7pm, my stomach was rumbling. I had waited too long to go get any food, when it's dark those Goblins have zero fear.

I threw on my shoes in a hurry, maybe I could make it to the closest gas station for some Cheetos or something.

When I opened the door to leave, I almost kicked over an open can of Spaghetti-O's. I picked up the can, along with the KitKat, 7up, and plastic spoon that my new friend left me.

Maybe we all could really change.

You know how everyone jokes around about wanting to be fed grapes like they're the king and shit?

That joke has always kind of annoyed me. I'd rather be eating grapes with my friends over them hand feeding them to me.

I asked Claire to hand feed me grapes one time, I came away from that encounter with a whole grape stuck up my left nostril.

It doesn't sound like much, sure, but it's enough to block the nasal passages and you can't blow it out. When you try to use your finger, you sort of smash it.

She's a mastermind of cruelties, and I love her.

I miss her.

This sucks massive ass.

The grape thing had a point though.

After yesterday I realized it wouldn't kill me to relax a little. I spend all day running around eating canned food and just being stressed. It can't be good for my health.

So, I went to Barnes and Noble and picked up some books about Bigfoot and planned to get enough canned food to last a few days.

I have also realized I can, in fact, take a trash bag somewhere on my food runs here and there.

When I was coming out of the store, I heard those little green pieces of shit making that squeaking sound they make.

Sure enough, here they came looking like Dobby's annoying green counterparts.

The goblins were really what I picture Rowling creating. She's an asshole and so are these things. I think I'd prefer spending a day with the goblins over Rowling though; these turds dislike everyone equally, they don't pinpoint one already marginalized group to attack from high up on their pop culture throne.

Fuck J.K. Rowling.

Remember when Stephen King tweeted out how much he loved her and everyone was like "no, not you!" and when he figured out why they said that he was like, "Yah, ok, nevermind. She's an asshole?"

Ranting about transphobic pieces of absolute horse dung aside; the little fuckers with their big ears were picking out little chunks of the surrounding buildings and plopping them into the striped one's mouth. The little tiger striped bag of crap was also being carried in a hammock by four other goblins.

He was the king with his grapes.

I think I'll call him Rowling from here on out.

Rowling was being a total prick. He was just lying there munching away at chunks of concrete like Cheeto's but still acting pissed. He made this weird sound that was like he was hacking up a loogie and sat up looking like a toddler who only got to watch baby shark fifteen times in one day when their average was sixteen. One of the goblins leading the party of seven climbed into the hammock with him and laid its head on his chest.

I don't want to describe the mating habits of goblins so I'll just tell you that from what I could see, he was a male, and the other was a female. There was… some hardware that confirmed this.

Ok, ok, I saw a goblin dick.

No, I don't really want to talk about how it grew out of a hole between his legs and looked like a gnarled old mold covered tree branch.

I think Rowling is the king turd of toilet bowl kingdom.

Bad metaphor.

He's the one in charge.
I'm going to have to kill him.

Some of these books I got are WILD.

The portals, the cloaking, the mental telepathy; some of it is spot on. But then some of it is bonkers.

It's like Ufology in a way; some of it you're nodding along like "yeah, hell yeah, this makes so much sense…" but then the next minute you're into some white supremacist racial elimination nonsense.

Nazis in Antarctica?

What the Hell does any of that have to do with Bigfoot?

I don't really know what exactly I'm talking about so I probably shouldn't be talking about it.

White supremacists are assholes.

Bigfoot, he doesn't seem to be an asshole.

I read for most of the day, which was odd.

Odd in the sense that yeah, I think at this point I know more about Bigfoot than anyone else; even these people who have spent years studying the species.

I just happened to fall into a stretch of bad luck and a flub in inter-dimensional travel that happened to put me here spending some real one on one bonding time with the guy.

The Expedition Bigfoot crew would be hella jealous, especially that Bryce Johnson guy. Hey, Bryce, you travelled to the jet ski dimension and took Michael and Riley with you, GET ME THE HELL OUT OF HERE PLEASE.

Isn't it weird how when we write in all caps it's like yelling? The quietest yelling you'll ever hear… or not hear, I guess.

Kind of like how I'm about to write I heard that Bigfoot could travel through dimensions from a book today, I didn't hear that. I have actually heard that with my ears before, but not today.

Tomorrow, I'm going to go out looking for my old pal; I want to see how his leg is doing and I need to ask about the dimensional travel stuff.

I cut out the picture of him stepping out of a portal at Skinwalker Ranch to show him. Maybe that particular Bigfoot is a distant cousin of my friend or something; and it's like in professional wrestling how people who are even associated with The Undertaker can teleport.

Help me Bigfoot, you're my only hope.

I've been making a huge mistake.

I thought Rowling was the biggest asshole still hanging around.

Turns out it's me.

I went back to the bookstore today; I guess I was really hoping Bigfoot was following me. I just sort of aimlessly flipped through magazines and kept my eyes out for those shithead little green things.

I was reading an article about Meghan Trainor and her husband; I already forgot his name. I was reading it because I think Meghan Trainor is the best. He was a Spy Kid; I do remember that much.

The article was about how they had side by side toilets together and the internet was calling them weird or something.

Let's get real here, if you've never sat on the floor while your partner uses the restroom after Taco Bell awaiting your turn, and so that neither of you will be lonely… I think your relationship may be failing.

The same with baths, gotta sit on the toilet lid while your partner bathes so that neither of you are alone.

I think M-Train and her Spy Kid husband have the right idea. Honestly, if I ever see Claire again and she hasn't found a better option than me, I'll ask her if she wants to install side by side toilets.

In high school we used to pass notes under the stalls to each other, not Claire and I, the other dudes. I don't know why we wouldn't just talk to each other. Everyone has this whole weird thing about pooping. It's like everyone is embarrassed for anyone else to know they poop… we all poop.

I used to get even weird about buying toilet paper, it's like an admittance of pooping. Which, just by existing I admit that right?

Now I'm all weirded out that I have written it down and someone may read it and find out the strange person who left these notes behind does in fact shit.

Anxiety is weird honestly.

I was startled mid-article by Bigfoot appearing beside me; that damn cloaking again.

I jumped and said, "gotta stop with the surprises, big guy."

He kind of squinted his eyes and frowned, let out this annoyed grumble.

He took the magazine from me and pointed to the Spy Kid, then tapped me on my chest. Then he pointed to Meghan Trainor and poked himself in the chest.

"No offense, you are a very nice-looking creature, but I don't think you look anything like M-Train. And I definitely don't look like the Spy Kid," I said, trying to break the news to him softly.

He lifted his arms in the air and clenched his fists, he was shaking them in annoyance. He turned the page to M-Train and Spy Kid kissing at their wedding or something; I hadn't read the article that far.

He pointed to Spy Kid, then me again.

He pointed to M-Train, and then himself again.

"See, mixed signals," I said, "because, again, I mean no offense here, you seem really cool and like one of the nicest Bigfoot I ever met… but I'm actually married, and I'm pretty sure there's laws against this type of thing. Also, I think Claire could kill us both at the same time, big guy-"

I didn't get to finish saying how she could take on like eighty Rowlings without breaking a sweat because Bigfoot picked me up and shook me by my shoulders.

I was terrified.

I thought human men were the worst about taking no for an answer.

He set me down and stormed off through the bookstore.

He came back with two cardboard cutouts, one was Harry Potter, the other was Princess Peach.

He sat Harry beside me, and then stood next to Princess Peach.

Me, again, an intellectual, didn't understand.

I shook my head in confusion.

He left again and came back with a men's fitness magazine and a women's fitness magazine.

He handed me the men's.

"Look, I get it, you're really strong, and you want a girlfriend I guess?" I said.

He fell forward onto his knees and lifted his arms like he was pleading to whatever god a Bigfoot worships.

"Sorry, I'm not really religious either," I said.

That was the bit that made him really agitated. He stood up and punched through the magazine shelf.

"Ok, ok! Sorry, big guy!" I said holding my hands up.

He threw Princess Peach at me, I ducked.

He threw the magazine at me as I was squatting, and it hit me on the head.

This must have knocked some common sense into the potato I'm working with as a brain because I realized.

"Ohhhhhhh," I said, "you get mad when I call you 'big guy' because you're not a guy! You're a woman!"

He, SHE jumped a little and let out a sigh of relief.

I did the same, I thought if I didn't pick up on the charades by the next example, I was going to be dead in a bookstore with the last bit of knowledge I put in my brain being about Meghan Trainor and her Spy Kid husband pooping side by side.

I totally blew it. I just assumed Bigfoot would be a guy; why couldn't Bigfoot be a she?

Actually, the Patterson Gimlin footage is a woman.

Ask Bryce Johnson and he'll tell you, "large, pendulous breasts."

I'm just a dumbass.

She lifted her head and sniffed the air before going Predator on me again.

I took the hint and hid, just in time to see a goblin come strolling in like it was there to pick up the five new books James Patterson released this month.

He must like the submarine books dads read.

The goblin sniffed the air and showed his teeth while backing up.

It grabbed an umbrella and pulled it back like a sword, its other hand sprouted those trademark claws.

When it tried to go through the door it accidentally popped open the umbrella, causing it to get jammed on the inside of the building while the goblin pulled in it from the outside.

This was a learning moment.

The goblin didn't even come into the store for the umbrella in the first place, so I have no idea why it was so determined to pull it through the doorway.

Seriously, it could have just dropped it and left.

Instead, the umbrella got pulled back into the building by an invisible force and then tossed to the ceiling with the goblin attached.

It looked like a little green Mary Poppins.

This place had two floors, and the second floor was up about as high as a third floor in a house.

The goblin flapped its arms like it was trying to fly; as it began its journey back down to the ground its eyes grew from softballs to basketballs.

Bigfoot wasn't invisible anymore and she was holding a piece of wooden shelving like a baseball bat. She swung with all her might, and I have to say, Babe Ruth would have been jealous. The Goblin's chest exploded on impact and weird green and blue blood followed its flight through the air. The store was coated in blood and random bits that fell from the things crushed midsection. It crashed through a window display, kept going across the side street, and hit the side of another building. It exploded like a water balloon leaving the wall to look like someone tried to make abstract art into graffiti and just spray-painted random covers all over it.

Bigfoot looked at me and her mouth turned into a slight gri

n.

I picked up the magazine I was reading-I wanted to finish that article goddamnit!-I headed out the front door and heard Bigfoot following me, we both looked at the remains of the goblin. I heard Bigfoot kind of giggle, but when I turned to look at her, she was already fading back into invisibility and heading away from me.

I looked at the smashed goblin and said, "if I were you, I'd wanna be me too. I'd wanna be me too."

I gotta find a good name for Bigfoot other than Bigfoot.

I thought about it all day.

What do you name Bigfoot?

It has to be something that defines how much of a bad ass she is.

Something short so that when we're on our goblin slaying adventures, I only have to say one syllable.

That's a daydream of mine; me and Bigfoot out here kicking ass.

Those little green fuckers don't stand a chance.

Then reality comes crashing back in when I remember how she cloaks herself when the goblins are close. It has to mean that the one off with Rowling wasn't a one off at all. I wonder how many times they've tried to kill one another.

Is she like Samara Weaving in the movie Ready or Not only instead of rich

Satanists she's dealing with goblins that eat concrete?

Which actually brings me to my next thought, one I've been dealing with every day but haven't written. Why are the goblins so hell bent on ripping us limb from limb? I don't want to eat their buildings. They can have all of them as long as they leave me a single roof covered place to sleep. I mean, that could even be a wooden home. Do they hate us the same way that we hate when a fly lands on a slice of pizza? Does my existence to them mean that their food has been used as a home?

Kind of weird to be on the flip side of that equation. Starting to think about how humanity as a whole has destroyed everything not-human's homes since we discovered how to breathe.

There's maybe something philosophical in here about how the goblins may be the exact thing we needed. They put us in our place. They showed us how it felt to be all the wildlife that we've displaced and harmed. Humanity is a walking plague; look at all the species we've forced into extinction.

Maybe the goblins hate me for that. maybe they're just mad I shit inside their food. Maybe they want to kill me, so they don't feel remorse for destroying another creature's home.

That last one would put the goblins in a more empathetic light than humanity; we don't even try to end any other species' suffering. In some weird, warped, comic villain way maybe the goblins are doing that; they've ruined my life and think it would be easier to kill me than watch me scuttle along suffering. That's showing some form of empathy, be it a grotesque and twisted version of it. Still, that shows they care more about other species than humans ever have. We take all of a species home, and just leave them to suffer.

Fuck you, Polar Bears! You don't need ice! Learn how to swim, dickhead!

Honestly, all of this pretending to be smart and reflecting aside; I think the goblins are just pure evil. They will kill everything and anything that steps in their path just for fun. So, another human characteristic; I won't get all fake smart and deep on that one.

I think I'm going to call Bigfoot Samara. Samara Weaving is a total bad ass, I can call her Sam for short, or Sammy when we're joking around.

I don't feel like going out today, so I'll go look for Sammy tomorrow.

I read in one of these books that Bigfoot communicates by hitting wood together; It's called wood knocking. I went back to the bookstore and broke a branch off one of the trees out front. I started hitting the tree with the stick hoping to hear my calls returned.

Samara wasn't answering.

She must have been letting me go to voicemail.

I really needed to check her leg, see how the stitches were holding up. It didn't seem to affect her too much when she got in that fight the other day.

Pretty one sided even with her injury.

I kicked around for a while trying to find something I could use to attract her.

I found some deer urine in an army surplus store. My stupid clumsy ass dropped it; the bottle busted open and splashed all over me. I got pissed off and kicked it. The bottle flew into a shelf with knives delicately displayed and sent them clattering to the floor.

I grabbed a backpack to put all of those in because at least then I could carry shit and have weapons.

I don't know why I've never thought to do this. I'm really starting to question if I'm even worth saving at this point. I could see the headlines now about my survival, "Man trapped in city with little monsters decides to carry plastic bags with cans of soup around with no means of defense."

I could have kept so much more food in this bag.

Fucking idiot.

After having this magical revelation in common sense, I heard the door open and that weird goblin chatter.

I squatted down behind a display for a tree stand. The thing was all set up like a little house. I watched through the window; the goblins were without Rowling. Must have been a small crew out and about in the daylight acting like assholes.

I still don't get it; I sleep at night; that's when they all come out and eat.

Why are they sometimes out in the daylight? Why are they bothering me?

One of them started sniffing the air, I was fucked. They can smell me out anywhere. It just kept sniffing though. It couldn't pinpoint what it smelled but it didn't like it.

I know that because its face scrunched up like it smelled a rotten fart and then it piled everywhere.

It was just gravel covered in blue slime.

The goblins sniffed some more and all barfed. They realized something in there was upsetting their tummies and decided to head out.

Now that they were gone, leaving me with blue slime covered gravel everywhere, I realized they must not like the smell of the chemically enhanced deer piss very much.

I grabbed the last five bottles from the shelf and headed home.

I'll use some like cologne tomorrow and try some more tree knocking.

Bigfoot came to me in the early hours of the morning just like she was an annoying neighbor that mows their lawn with the sunrise. The one with the weed whacker is always the absolute worst. Especially if it hits against a fence. It sounds like someone took a bicycle with a card in the spokes and attached a racecar engine to it.

She woke me up by shoving me off the bed. I don't know how she keeps getting in here when I lock the door. I need to explain to her it's kind of rude.

I thought about trying to explain it when I noticed she was crying. She was standing beside the bed with tears running down her face; the trail they were leaving was messing with her cloaking so she just had these weird invisible spots she would sniff and wipe away.

I stood up and sat on the edge of the bed; I motioned for her to do the same.

When she sat down, she started making this whine sound that was so high pitched I could barely hear it. Like a dog whistle turned down one decibel. It made my chest hurt.

"What's going on?" I asked, as if she was just going to magically start speaking.

She pointed to her head, tapped on mine, and then held out her hand.

I put my hand in hers, it started to tingle, and I could feel my brain slowing way down.

When I looked at her to ask what was going on I was somewhere else.

I was in a forest watching a smaller version of herself, a goblin sized version, run and jump at another Bigfoot. The smaller one collided with the bigger one's midsection, the larger fell over like it got shot by a canon and started making a sound I can only describe as laughter.

I felt happiness, serenity, peace, all course through my body.

This was Samara's family.

In a flash I watched as the other Sasquatch was holding hands with a man in a black suit, I could see behind them another man was sitting on a log playing some form of wooden board game with the child. I watched as the man and the other Sasquatch let go of each other's hands; the man said, "thank you, we'll make sure none of this happens again," and then I was somewhere else.

I was in the Newport Music Hall, watching as Samara's partner helped guide a team of men in building the portal device. He touched a crystal that was built into it, and it looked like he sent all of his energy into the stone. The stone glowed green as it was hoisted into the air.

Then the scene changed again, and I was back in the woods running behind the other Bigfoot. As I followed, I looked to both sides and saw the goblins running faster than us; they were going to get in front of us. A green light filled the forest, and I could see a circle in the distance; it looked like someone cut out a piece of the night and put a brightly lit forest in its place. Other Bigfoot were stepping through in a hurry. One that was covered in grey hair was holding the portal open and letting the others step through.

I looked to my sides again and clearly the goblins would cut me and my family off.

I felt anger, frustration, sadness. I reached out and grabbed this massive tree limb; holding it like a spear I planted it into my partner's back and shoved as hard as I could. It worked like a pool stick and shoved him hard enough that he moved just fast enough to make it past the spot where the goblins cut off our path.

He kept running; he handed our young to the grey Bigfoot and turned back. He could see I was cut off; I knew he would sacrifice himself to save me.

Our child needed at least one parent; the community wouldn't be enough.

I felt an image leave my head and transport into his mind; the image of our child, surrounded by the community, all of them mourning with the child.

He nodded; I could see tears running across his face.

He turned and went through the portal with the elder and the child.

I was back in my own body with the sense that somewhere in the forests of Ohio there was a pile of around sixteen dead goblins.

I put my hand on Samara's shoulder as she cried.

When she looked at me, I tapped her head, then mine, and said, "can you do that in reverse?"

She held out her hand and when I took it, I felt memories leaving my head.

The most important times with Claire; our wedding day, negative pregnancy test after negative pregnancy test, trips to hundreds of doctors to find out what was wrong, standing at her father's grave as she cried and said he was a son of a bitch that deserved it, standing at my parents' grave as I cried and she said they didn't deserve to be taken so soon, then the day of the portal mishap.

She let go of my hand, she placed her massive hand on my shoulder.

"We're in the same boat here, Samara," I said, "oh, I hope you're ok with that name."

She grinned a little; for once I felt like I made a decent decision with her.

She lay back and fell asleep before I could say anything else.

I went to the small loveseat and slept.

When we woke up, she was showing me pages in one of the Bigfoot books about how Sasquatch can create portals. Then she went and picked up the empty coke bottle from the night before. She filled it with water and held it to her face. It started to glow green.

She then pointed to me, then the portal, then to both our heads.

So, I guess tomorrow we're going to go and try to restart the portal.

Goddamnit.

Goddamnit.

GODDAMNIT.

I'm sitting here on a concrete floor in a jail cell.

Tape scratch, rewind, how did I get here?

We went to the Newport the next morning; we were all stocked up on weapons that we could use. I had this big ass machete I found in the army surplus store, and Samara had a crowbar.

We didn't know if we would encounter goblins, but I assumed it would be best to play it safely.

Good choice too.

The Newport Music Hall is a smallish venue. When you walk in, you're in one large room. There's the stage in front, and a lowered floor in the middle for all the "moshers."

It was filled with green.

Green bodies piled onto green bodies.

Rowling was sitting atop the pile, some of the bodies forming a throne below him.

His eyes were open, and he stared at us.

He groaned and stood up, walking across the sleeping bodies like Jesus walking on the surface of the water. I didn't need convincing; I was a believer in his unholy and vile powers.

He dropped his claws, and his face formed a small grin.

We were fucked and he knew it.

He made a clicking noise with his mouth and all of the goblins opened their eyes.

Have you ever seen the remake of Willard?

You know the scene with the elevator?

That's what it looked like.

They swarmed around and over him like a green tidal wave filled with knives.

Samara and I swung our weapons hard and fast. She would take out five with one swoop and I had to work on one at a time.

She did cut one of them in half with the dull side of the crowbar, that made me pause for a minute because that's bad ass.

Not even ten seconds into the attack it stopped, and all the goblins ran away.

They fled through the second level, out of doors, windows, and some running right past us.

Rowling was lying face down in the middle of the lowered floor with a dart sticking out of his neck.

I started to say “what the hell…” when Samara fell in front of me with three in her neck.

Then all I remember is waking up in a jail cell.

To my left, Samara faded into sight for a second so I could see her, then faded away.

To my right, Rowling stared at me with malice.

All three of us were in separate jail cells.

Rowling hissed at me, and I flipped him off.

“Fuck you, Rowling,” I said.

A door in the room opened and a guy in a red MAGA hat came in. His shirt had a massive Q on it.

“Oh, fucking great,” I said. I knew exactly what this guy was about.

“We knew you’d lead us to your reptilian overlords,” he said. “We’ve been following you for a week or more. We couldn’t decide why you stayed behind while all the other people went. Then we knew. You’re the traitor. You’re the one that sold us to the reptilians.”

I looked over at Rowling, who was now facing the Q man, we both made eye contact and for once I felt a kinship with the goblin. He was just as confused as I was.

"We thought the reptilians would be taller," he said pointing to Rowling. "We also had a hunch the Sasquatch were helping them."

"Ok," I said, "you're fucking crazier than a shark in an elementary school swimming pool. First, that is a Hopkinsville Goblin, not a reptilian. Second, if you've been following us you have had to have seen us fighting them."

He stared ahead.

"Classic Q'Anon stupid dumb ass idiot moron," I said. "Only looked at like one percent of the picture and based your whole belief system around it."

He leapt forward and put a handgun through the bars and screamed in my face, "I know you! You're working for Killary, Brandon, and the Hollywood elite. How much did they pay you? What promises did they make? Why did you convince everyone that going through the portal was a path to safety?"

He pulled the gun out and calmed down.

This guy was an anti-vax dipshit in 2020, and an anti-portal dipshit in 2027.

Samara faded into sight and stared at him. I thought Rowling's stare was harsh.

"What do you want, ugly?" Q man said. "What did you stand to gain? We knew the reptilian home world was on the other side of that portal. We know they're factory farming all the humans who fell for this. But what do you get? The whole planet?"

Samara just stared at him.

She was pissed.

This guy was lucky there were bars there separating him from a life without limbs.

He threw my notebook at me, and a pen.

"Write the new gospel," he said. "The Q testament!"

With that he banged on the door, when it opened, he stepped through and turned back to yell, "WHERE WE GO AS ONE, WE GO AS MANY!"

Rowling stuck his arm through the bars and pointed the sternest middle finger I had ever saw at the guy.

"Looks like we're all stuck together," I said.

Rowling looked toward Samara and I and nodded.

I was woken up today by the lasers coming from Rowling's eyes and burrowing deep writhing my flesh. They went so deep I could feel them in my bone marrow.

That's how powerful his stare was.

We led a group of far-right conspiracy theorists right into their home, so yeah, I could see why he was pissed at me.

I didn't think it was necessary how he kept trying to piss on me from his cell instead of using the toilet, but I guess one does as one does. It's not my place to kink shame anyone.

Samara just sat in her cell and stared ahead at the doorway. She was in more grief than Rowling and me. We were spending our time being children and taunting each other; Samara was just sitting there stewing in her anger and sadness.

A new man in a "Let's go Brandon" shirt came in today. Rowling rolled his big black eyes and let out an annoyed sigh. These people are apparently even a nuisance to inter-dimensional goblins.

"You're coming to meet Gary today," the man said while he unlocked my cell.

"Gary?" I said. "You're basically an evil villain organization and your leader is named Gary?"

"We don't choose our names."

"Yeah, but, come on. You could have changed it to something like Racist-Rick or something."

My sentence was dotted with a punch in my face. My head hit Samara's cell; she stood up and moved to the bars. The man held up a massive gun of some sort and pointed it at her.

I don't know guns.

It was big and looked like something from *Call of Duty*.

"You know what this does right?" he said while pointing the gun at Samara.

She backed off and sat back down. Then the dick pointed it at me and told me that they weren't racists; their beliefs that African Americans should be happy they were enslaved is being misunderstood.

His words, not mine.

I firmly believe this is racist and he is an asshole.

We walked down a hallway and into what I took to be an interrogation room. It looked like one from TV, so I ran with it.

I gave the mirror the bird just like every cool guy that gets arrested in a movie.

"No one is behind that," said a voice behind me. "We don't play games and tell lies like your people."

"Who are my people?" I asked.

"Those who serve the reptilians."

"…ok."

"Tell us what we want to know."

"What do you want to know?"

"Why?"

"Why what?"

"You know why you're here."

"I genuinely don't."

"You do."

"I don't."

"You do."

"I. Do. Not."

"Tell me why?"

"Why what?"

"Why did you sell out the human race, you son of a bitch!?"

"Let's just say I did do whatever you're accusing me of. Don't you think it's a little weird I'm here all alone, no one to protect me, no army. I'm just out here eating cans of peaches and avoiding the same green little shitbags as you."

"They must have turned on you."

"Are you having a laugh? Are you ok?"

He slammed his palms on the table at this one; then flipped it when I asked if I could have a glass of water. He's seen some movies with interrogation rooms too apparently.

"WHO DO YOU WORK FOR?!" he screamed in my face; I got my glass of water in the form of his spit all over me.

I shrugged my shoulders; I didn't even have a funny joke to make.

He looked at the mirror and waved toward me. About ten seconds later I was being escorted from the room by two new dudes in red hats while I yelled, "I thought there wasn't anyone in there huh? You're a fraud! A phoney! A fake!"

It was a productive moment.

I was tossed back into my cell hard enough that I conked my head on the toilet.

It made a hollow sound like when you drop a frying pan.

Rowling pissed at the men and laughed as they fled; then he turned around to sit and stare lasers at me again.

Samara was looking at me wanting some form of explanation. All I could say was, "I have no idea what just happened."

The food is shit.

This red hat slid a plate of noodles to me under my cell. It was Alfredo; but it had a BBQ swirl on top.

What kind of a God would force me to eat Alfredo with BBQ sauce? Is this how they plan to torture me?

Nope. I found that out when Gary came back.

He had a portable DVD player.

That son of a bitch bastard from Hell.

"Got some stuff for you to watch," he said as he popped in a DVD and sat the player on the ground in front of my cell.

It was a documentary about the reptilian overlords.

"See," he said pointing at Rowling. "That little guy looks nothing like these. His face is all smooshed up like a pug. Is he a juvenile? Is he the antichrist?"

"He is an asshole," I said, "but I don't think he's smart enough to be the antichrist."

We both looked over in time to see Rowling dangling a big line of green snot from his finger to his mouth before slurping it up.

Gary gagged.

I just thought it was par for the course and went on.

The video played, all the biggies of the right-wing conspiracies were there; baby eating, the Hollywood elite, the Illuminati, JFK Jr., Nazis on the moon, the Covid vaccine turning people into liquid for reptilians like some deranged Capri-Sun, white replacement theory, the feminist agenda, you know, all the bullshit these idiots use to make themselves look like the oppressed instead of the oppressors.

"What's the point here, Gary?" I asked.

"Don't you see?"

"I wouldn't have asked if I understood."

"They're here to eliminate all straight white males."

"I'm a straight white male."

"You should be concerned."

"Yet… here I am… completely unbothered. I think that's because I'm not a racist-sexist-dipshit-moron-AHHHHHHHHHHHHHHH!"

I let out a scream because he was tazing my ass!

The world was on fire, I was covered in electric eels.

"Had Ray take off the governor," Gary said, "or whatever. Now it's like a cattle prod."

He pointed it at Samara who showed him her teeth and squinted her eyes.

"Yeah," he said, "I'm sure if you weren't in there, I wouldn't have any arms to use this."

I heard the sound of rocks being smashed together; Rowling was eating a chunk of the wall like it was a cheeseburger.

Gary hit him with the taser.

Rowling shook for a minute before ripping the wire from his body. He dove at the bars of the cage and reached his kitchen knife talons through.

His talons were so sharp, so fast, that I swear he was cutting through atoms.

Gary backed away to the door and shook his head. He came back over to the DVD player and pushed a few buttons.

The words "repeat all" came across the screen, then he left for more pleasant company.

This is why I've been sitting here watching this documentary for six hours.

I woke up to yelling and the smell of burnt hair.

I rolled over in a hurry and saw that two men had Samara's arm pulled through the bars of her cell. A third man held a lighter.

"WHY ARE YOU HELPING THEM?" lighter man screamed as the other two pulled harder on the ropes.

Samara let out a groan that grew into a deep bellow.

It made my stomach turn.

I heard Rowling shriek beyond me when she did it.

Lighter guy didn't hesitate. He flicked the lighter to Sam's fur. Her whole body lit up like your Christmas sweater did when your annoying cousin thought it was funny how the fire spread over it quickly and vanished. Only Samara didn't know any of these guys' moms, and she couldn't speak the same language to rat them out about the pack of cigarettes they kept behind the garage.

They yelled some more, Samara let out the same noise; only this time it morphed into more of a cry. I could see her flashing back and forth between visibility, and invisibility; which pissed the men off even more.

"Light 'eem up! He's trying to get away! Tell-ee-poor-tay-shun!" one yelled while lighter man hit her with the small flame again.

I jumped hard at the bars of my cell; I felt the bruise already growing in my chest where I hit it so hard. "Fucking quit, you racist booger-dicks! She can't speak like us!" I yelled.

The men grabbed my arm then.

They pulled it through and singed the hair on my arms while asking me things I couldn't comprehend through the anxiety of burning.

One of the men screamed like he put his hand on a hot burner.

Samara had him in a choke hold through the bars and he was already turning purple.

The other two men pulled handguns and pointed them at her.

She let out a roar that made my head feel like it was filled with hundred-pound weights.

I yelled at them to stop, I yelled for her to stop.

Time sort of froze, I put my hand on

her shoulder through the bar and pleaded with her to calm down.

Eventually the tension released as the man was dropped into a pile on the floor.

"We're coming back tomorrow. And we just aren't going to be friendly then," they said as they slammed the door.

I looked over at Rowling, who was surprisingly quiet throughout these events. He was covered in feathers. Can't make this up. The men had covered him in something sticky, maybe glue, and then covered him in feathers.

He looked like the world's most dangerous chicken.

After the incident yesterday I think all three of us were on high alert.

Anytime the door moved we would jerk back like pain was coming our way. No one ever came back. That was the worst torture, feeling like someone was coming through the door only for nothing to happen. It was like holding a shit for too long.

I didn't sleep. I guess sleeping isn't going to be a thing I get too much of when a goblin is right beside you eating concrete. He's figured out he can eat around the bars in the back of the cell, and no one notices. I don't know how his claws are digging into solid concrete, but I am also not here to question it.

When someone finally showed up to bother us today, it was the same redshirt fuck as my first day; the same with the lighter. This may be an accurate sign as to how many of them are in here.

He made me leave the room again.

"What's your name?" I asked.

"That's not really any of your business," he said as he open-handed slapped me across the face.

What was the point of that?

To hurt my pride?

Establish dominance?

I was in too much shock to even be pissed off about it.

"Ok," I said, "I know who Gary is now. I know yesterday was the asshole duo and that shitty first guy I met. Which one of them is Ray?"

"Ray never leaves the garage."

"Five. There are only five of you, am I right?"

"Shut the fuck up."

"The F-word tells me I hit the nail on the head there."

"Shut the fuck up, Killary following swine."

"Let's go Brandon."

"You're learning."

He opened the door to the same damn interrogation room and shoved me in. I knew the drill at this point, so I just grabbed my seat and waited.

In comes Gary; this time he was carrying a tea pot.

I thought that was very nice of him until the other two men followed him in and held my hand palm up while Gary dripped boiling hot water into it. They let me go and shoved me over backwards in the chair.

When I stood up to retaliate three guns were pointing at me.

"What the fuck is the deal, you two?" I asked. "This dude tells you to torture someone, and you say 'Yah, good idea'? Y'all need to listen to Meghan Trainor and learn how to say one specific word."

They stared at me like I had just told them I wiped my ass with the constitution.

"No," I said, "my name is-NO, my sign is-NO… not fans I guess?"

Gary nodded and they were on me; they were the starving Great White, and I was the wounded Seal.

They kicked, punched, and I swear to God above one of them bit me.

When they stopped, I looked at the spot where I thought I was bitten and saw bloody spots in the form of a bite mark in my inner right arm. I held it up and said, "why did you bite me?"

"That's an easy one," Gary finally graced me with his voice, "had to see if you had bones."

"Do fucking what now?"

"If you had the vaccine, you wouldn't have bones. You would be a bag of liquid walking around waiting to be drained."

"That makes sense."

I was firmly placed in my seat by the dynamic duo as Gary slid a picture across the table.

"Do you know who that is?" He asked.

"It's Kyle Rittenhouse, a famous racist dickhead that got away with murder," I said.

"A patriot. A hero. A goddamn savior of freedom."

"An asshole. A racist. A piece of shit."

Gary didn't like my description, so he nodded, and I got punched in the back of the head.

I turned around and made eye contact with red shirt number two and frowned.

"You don't talk about a patriot that way in front of me, mother fucker," Gary said.

"I was talking about a worthless shit stain that exists on the very fabric of existence," I said as I closed my eyes waiting for the punch that never came.

"You really are loyal to the reptilians, aren't you?"

"Gary, look, let's just spill it. What the fuck do you think is going on? You tell me and I'll tell you how right or wrong you are."

"The BLM movement was a distraction."

"BELT LOOPS MATTER," spoke the other two in unison like it was a military chant. If I didn't still think I would be shot; I would have beat the shit and three bucks out of those racist fucks.

"I didn't know the military had a racist asshole branch," I said, "what's it called? The racist force? The Fucking-Stupid-Should-Be-Sent-Into-Space-For-Being-Worthless-Asshole-Rines?"

"None of us were in the military. We refuse to put ourselves in a position where we could be forced to serve the reptilians."

"Cops then?"

"Just average patriots."

"Are there five of you?"

"We know after the distraction, your scientists opened portals and allowed the reptilians in. They pretended to eat all of us; when really, they were herding us into their home world so they could farm us."

"Ok. I'll give you that considering reality, that doesn't sound quite as crazy, but what does this Kyle asshole have to do with anything?"

"He was killed by a reptilian when the portals opened."

"Good fucking riddancehouse."

"What?"

"Rittenhouse, Riddancehouse, get it?"

"This conversation is a waste of my time. Clearly, you would be better off with a nice drink."

The two goons held my head back and forced my mouth open as Gary held the water above. He slowly let one droplet drip into my throat. I could feel the skin bubble. I screamed and tried to get free. In the process my untied hands flapped around like a bird's wings, and I hit one of the idiots in the nuts.

When his grip loosened, I stood up and punched Gary in the face as hard as I possibly could. When he was falling, I grabbed the kettle and turned to the other standing man. I pulled back my arm to splash him with the water when I felt like I got shot in the back. I went down hard; I was lucky enough that my reflexes made me toss the kettle across the room.

"GODDAMNIT, GAVIN. CAN'T YOU DO ANYTHING RIGHT?" I heard a new voice.

"Sorry, Ray. I didn't expect him to piss me off so badly."

"All of you need to chill the fuck out immediately," this was another new voice. I rolled my head and saw a pair of boots with the confederate flag printed all over them in the doorway. "This guy doesn't know anything. He's not smart enough to be this good of an actor."

The boots walked toward me; one pulled back and kicked me hard in the stomach. I rolled over onto my back and stared up into the face of a new person. This man had three scars running across his face, probably from a goblin. He was sporting a white hat covered in bloodstains, it read "Fuck Joe Biden, and fuck you for voting for him."

He squatted down and looked right

into my eyes; I could see there was a brain behind his. A brain that could have been smart until too many Newsmax and YouTube conspiracy theories turned it into Mountain Dew Jell-O.

"Don't try to joke with me, bitch," he said, "I'll beat the shit out of you. I don't have time for bullshit."

"Is that why you have Gavin pretend to be you? Or is that because of your fucked up face?" I asked. The only response I got was punched in the face.

"One question," I said through bloody lips, "you all call Joe Biden Brandon. But then you say, 'let's go Brandon', so wouldn't that mean you're actually cheering for him."

Gary, the real Gary, grabbed ahold of my bottom lip with a pair of pliers that he seemed to manifest out of thin air. He pulled my lip out so far I thought it would tear away from my face, but then he ran a pocket knife across it lightly enough to just cause a small trickle of blood.

"You better get used to the taste of your own blood," he said.

"You forgot my lips were already bleeding," I said.

The two men held me down and opened my mouth again; at this point I was wondering when this relationship would transition to me at least getting dinner before they pretended to be demented dentists.

Gary grabbed my tongue with the pliers and kept squeezing until my body had no choice but to scream out.

When he let go of my tongue he whispered in my ear, "you're good with your tongue. Maybe I should take your only means of self-defense. You don't have an amendment guarding that."

I spit blood in his face.

The two men again went to torture me. This time Gary lifted his hand in a pause gesture. He waved goodbye to me and the next thing I knew I was being dragged through the building back to the cell.

They threw me in the cell hard and I hit my head on the toilet again.

"Whoa, what happened to his face?" Lighter man was in there; he held a hose and pointed it at Rowling's cell. Rowling wasn't covered in feathers anymore; they were in a wet pile in the corner. His skin was steaming though, so I assumed the old hot water trick.

One of the dynamic duo said something to lighter man and they left in a hurry.

I looked to Samara and said, "Six, there are only six of them."

She nodded and stared at the door.

I heard the all too familiar sound of concrete mashing together.

Rowling was feasting.

I went over to the bar he was eating

around and pulled it toward me. He had eaten enough around it that there was a space big enough he could fit through into my cell.

We made eye contact, and he started frantically digging into the concrete around the bar.

I don't know who was stupider; us for not figuring this out sooner, or the Q's for just being them. Either way, the next day, we were out of there.

We have had a doozy of a day.

I'll start from when I woke up.

I could not tell you if it was today, or late-night last night.

I woke up facing Samara's cell; the sound of metal hitting concrete was one hell of an alarm.

I rolled over halfway and came face to face with Rowling. He was just standing over me staring down. I thought he wanted me to see him and understand I was dead before he started ripping into me.

I was all of a sudden very aware of the fact that his claws could cut through solid concrete.

Luckily for me, my skin, my bones, and maybe Claire if she ever wants to see me again; he stepped over me.

He started digging as fast as he could.

Before long he was able to pull the bar out enough that he slipped through.

Samara stood to her full height and showed her teeth to him. Rowling flexed his claws and squatted like he was ready to fight.

"Hey, dickheads," I said, "let's get out of here first and then you can kill each other."

Rowling slowly changed his claws from death machine to digging machine. He started frantically digging at the bars near the front of the cage.

When I tell you I was so pissed to see it only took ten minutes; why hadn't he done this in the first place?

He popped his little body through and tried the door handle; it was locked of course.

Using his one last thought for the day, he squatted down on the side of the door so that when it opened, he would be blocked.

I got tired of waiting when I saw the sun coming up, so I started screaming.

"Go invisible," I said to Samara. I spoke frantically because this part of my plan was crucial, and I guess I must have thought she could read my mind to figure it out.

Have I mentioned that I'm not that great of a planner?

She went invisible.

Rowling looked at me and nodded.

He knew what I was doing and judging by how his claws stretched out, he was ready for a fight.

The door flew open and Fake-Gary/Gavin came in. He was wearing a shirt that had Lauren Boebart in a bikini—the top was an American flag, and the bottom was the confederate— she was holding some sort of gun and waving a MAGA flag. Two heads were pinned below her high heeled foot, Alexandria Ocasio-Cortez and Ilhan Omar.

I didn't even say anything, I just gave him the sternest middle finger I possibly could.

"Yeah," he said, "good morning to you too."

He noticed the two empty cells and took a few steps back to the door before turning and running.

The dynamic duo and Lighter man came back with guns ready. Lighter man shoved his between the bars of my cell and yelled, "WHERE THE FUCK DID THEY GO?"

I lied and said they sort of teleported and left me behind. He bought it.

He nodded at one of the duo who stepped forward and unlocked Samara's cell. He poked his gun in and looked around. When he turned to shrug, that's when they realized they were fucked.

Samara faded back into visibility.

She grabbed the man by his head and lifted him up just in time for his body to become riddled with bullet holes from the other two. They stopped shooting and started backing up toward the door.

That's where they met the sharpened blades of the world's most bad-ass lawnmower.

Rowling sliced at Lighter man's calves, eventually he fell forward with no legs below him. He used his hands to try and crawl away. He only got a few feet before Rowling was on him again; his claws sliced through the body like they were made of lava and the body was made of ice.

The man Samara had was being pulled through the bars of her cell; his bones were breaking; limbs were tearing from their place. When his skull came through, I puked.

Gavin was gone so fast he left burn marks on the ground.

Within a half a minute the crawling guy's head was being used to prop the door open.

Samara walked through the open door and fell forward crying out in pain.

Rowling had lived up to his name and behaved as an asshole once again.

He moved like a flash, only pausing at the open doorway to look back and give us one of those all too well-known sneers. That look said, "yah, sorry 'bout this, but fuck you."

He turned and ran down the hallway; he ran past a door just as it opened, and three other men came through; Gavin, Ray, and lighter man.

Samara's leg was bad. Instead of one bad slash she had three this time, and they were deeper.

The three men trained their guns on her as they surveyed the mess of dirty laundry their friends and companions had turned into.

Samara was quick, she swiped her arm out at lighter man's leg and swung him through the other two. His head hit the concrete wall and exploded like that watermelon I threw off a bridge onto the roof of a passing train.

She grabbed Gavin by his god-awful shirt and threw him my direction. He landed right in front of my cell, and I took the opportunity to say, "that is the worst shirt I have ever seen in my life," before I started hitting him with the bottom of my fist through the bars.

Samara was facing Ray, who had now pulled out some manipulated lighter that shot flames like a mini flamethrower.

Who the fuck was this guy? MacGyver?

Gavin grabbed my fist and pulled my arm through the bars. My head smashed against them rattling my teeth and vision.

I heard Ray screaming and looked over in time to see Samara's fur get covered in flames and do that Christmas sweater effect again. She was prepared for it; she had stepped through the blaze to grab the man's arm. An arm, which by the way, flew through the air and thunked against the side of Fake-Gary's skull.

I grabbed the lighter from the severed arm and pointed it at Gavin's mouth; he opened his mouth to scream just as I opened the flame and cooked the inside of his mouth and throat like a hot dog at a Boy Scout camp.

He stopped screaming and lay there, the place that used to hold his tongue was now a mess of blackened flesh, burnt teeth, and a tongue that looked like it was cooked up for dinner.

Again, I puked.

After I finished emptying my already empty stomach, I found keys on Gavin and opened the cell.

Samara was sitting down with her back against the wall. She was holding her injured leg again.

I helped Samara stand up, nearly falling over the pile of gore that was formerly named Ray. I assumed that it was Ray because that pile of nasty wasn't there a little bit ago, and Ray was now MIA. I get the feeling we probably wouldn't see Ray and that pile in the same room.

We made our way through the jail on guard expecting the real Gary to leap out at any second.

He never did.

We did find enough first aid materials that I was able to spend most of the day fixing Samara's wounds again.

When her wounds were sewn shut, we did another sweep of the building to make sure Gary wasn't hiding.

All we found was a missing cop car and an empty spot on the wall where the keys would be hanging.

We didn't travel back to my hotel room, that was too far. We went across the street to a mattress store.

You ever notice how many of those there are? Surely no one is buying enough mattresses to keep that place in business.

We're going to rest tonight, then tomorrow try and get as close to the portal again as we can.

I slapped myself in the head as hard as I could and exclaimed, "the deer piss!"

Samara actually jumped out of shock. I somehow said something so damn random that I scared Bigfoot for once, and not the other way around.

"Samara," I said, "those little bastards HATE the smell of deer piss. Like, they absolutely loathe it. One of them puked instantly. If we can get to a store and find some, we can pour it all over ourselves and get to the portal without surfing the waves of clawed green assholes."

She nodded and then kept walking down the street.

I kept making the turns I knew, kept going the only way I knew how to get us to a department store that was on the way back to the hotel.

At some point I realized the hotel wasn't really relevant anymore. I have my bag, I have the notebook still, I can do without some of that stuff.

We made it to a Walmart in pretty quick time; it only took around an hour of walking. When we went in the store, I explained to Samara that we better do a quick walk through and make sure we were truly alone.

I made a lap around one side, and she did the other. When we met at the back of the store by the entrance to the back rooms, she was carrying Slim-jim and happily munching away.

"Isn't that the wrong brand?" I asked.

She shrugged and kept chewing; I don't think she got the joke.

We looked through all the offices and the break room. Clean. The break room smelled slightly like old Hot Pockets and depression though. Which is totally valid. If there is a Hell, it's probably just Walmart.

We went into the back area that was used for unloading the trucks. Massive metal racks were on all sides, filled with boxes of merchandise.

I found the aisle with the boxes for sporting goods and sure enough; our luck paid off. There sat two giant boxes of deer urine. All we would have to do is get a cart and wheel them out.

First things first, I was starving and the food I had been eating was absolute shit. We went and found some snacks, ate in the electronics area while I told Samara about the movies on the shelves. She wasn't really interested in my knowledge about the Child's Play franchise, but she nodded along and humored me.

We searched the sporting goods area and found more deer piss. We also found a bunch of knives and guns. I don't even know how to load a gun and when I asked Samara she broke the glass, grabbed a rifle, and swung it like a baseball bat.

No guns for us I suppose.

We got two shopping carts and loaded them full of whatever we thought we would need. Then, I was about worn out, so we took two display futons off the shelves and laid down.

I tried telling her all about Claire; but I heard some deep snoring and decided I should do the same.

The first thing I thought when I woke up was, *I didn't know we were in the presence of a goblin with forklift certification.*

The little green fucker was driving the thing with a purpose. Shelves were getting demolished, merchandise was getting smashed; I even saw a copy of classic action movie starring Keanu Reeves, Speed, get crushed under the tires.

Personally, I like Keanu. I don't understand this problem a lot of people have with him. He's a pretty good actor and it seemed like he really hit his stride in John Wick. Was Dracula a little rough? Oh yeah. But that's just my opinion.

The thing kept driving around, smashing shit; two other goblins were running around beside it and swinging from the forks in the front. At one point the forklift turned too quickly and smacked one of the two goblins out of the air. It slid across the floor, then stood up and let out the loudest shriek I have ever heard before swinging from the forks and launching itself onto a shelf with TVs.

It started knocking them off the shelf in time for the forklift to drive over them.

One tv got stuck under the wheels and just got pushed forward; it grinded into the concrete and made the worst sound I think plastic can possibly make.

The driver wasn't paying attention to where it was going, focusing way too heavily on the TV, and it crashed through a rack of CDs, then slammed right into the display case for video games.

The three goblins thought that was hilarious. They just laughed and rolled on the ground.

The driver hopped out and dug his claws into the concrete floor; it pulled up a chunk and started chowing down.

Samara and I just stayed on our futons in silence and watched it all, hoping they wouldn't notice us.

That hope was short lived. The concrete eater looked in our direction and its jaw dropped. Broken up concrete poured out like half chewed spaghetti.

He was upsetti-spaghetti.

It made a shriek, and the forklift was pulled up beside it by one of the others.

The driver jumped forward through the little opening and swung by the forks again while the original driver hopped in.

I had enough time to start to ask myself where the third one was, but I was interrupted by the third one shrieking right beside my ear.

I fell off the futon, rolled across the ground and hit Samara's shins. She was already standing up and pissed.

She was holding her futon up in the air like a weapon, and then slammed it down hard onto the goblin. The thing was there one second, and then the next it was a pile of tangled metal and weirdly colored goo.

One down two to go.

The forklift screeched its tires and drove at us faster than something NASCAR related that I don't have the capacity to think of right now. We both jumped out of the way and watched as it drove its forks through a box of pillows.

The goblin that was on the forks was now on top of the forklift. Somehow, it had acquired a frying pan in its short journey and decided now would be a good time to throw it at us.

Samara caught it by the handle and spun around like she was throwing a discus. When she let go, it hit the goblin square in the chest and sent it flying off the roof and into another set of shelves.

The forklift backed up and spun; the goblin made this happen so quickly I was positive we missed something in our search yesterday and this was a regular occurrence in this store. It flew past us as we both dodged and ran down opposite aisles. I looked back to make sure Samara was ok, she was cloaking and climbing a shelf.

I ran as fast as I could down the aisles and found myself somehow in the grocery area. I turned down an aisle that was filled with jars of pickles and ran to the end hoping to get to the milk coolers and hide in the back.

I was met at the end of the aisle by the forklift. I turned and ran back into the aisle as it chased me. I could hear the jars smashing on the ground as they fell off the shelf. I heard another sound, the sound of all the jars on top of the shelf being shattered on the roof of the forklift.

I ran across a large aisle and found myself in the clothing area. I jumped sideways out of the forklifts path as it drove headfirst into the dressing room. I looked back at the pickle aisle and saw a cloaked Samara jump off the top shelf and fly over my head.

I had no idea she was also super-jumping-foot.

She landed on the roof of the forklift, reached in through the side and grabbed the goblin's head like an orange.

The goblin kicked and slashed out at her, she just grunted and threw the thing like a baseball toward the front of the store. It hit one of the cash registers and bounced before thudding against the brick wall up front.

A dull thud rang out and Samara frowned. She turned around and lifted the other goblin above her head. The thing was still holding the frying pan.

She slammed it down into the ground so hard I swear there is probably a crater where it hit.

After both of us sat on the ground breathing heavy and trying to regain our composure from living through a forklift certified goblin, we gathered the two shopping carts we wanted to take and left the insanity of the store.

We walked a few miles and got as close as I felt comfortable being to the Newport before we took our carts into another Mattress Firm. Seriously why are there so many? Tomorrow we're going to head to the portal and get the fuck out of here.

Of all the things I've seen, heard, or done over the past couple weeks; finding out there's an elaborate tunnel system under Mattress Firm used to transport aliens is something I didn't have on my end of the world bingo card.

"Is that sasquatch?"

That's what we were asked by this odd little man eating a fudgesicle.

I stopped pushing my cart out the door and looked at Samara.

She rolled her eyes and turned around to the guy.

He walked toward her with his hand extended for a shake saying, "oh my god I've seen videos, but I never thought I'd see you in real life. Desmond, my name is Desmond. Who is that?"

He nodded at me while shaking Samara's hand.

"Jim Tiptree. That's Samara," I explained.

"Really? You're hanging out with sasquatch and your last name is Tiptree?"

"Alright, well, we really should be going. It's been nice to meet you but-"

"Wanna see how a five-foot tall, one-hundred-pound black guy stayed alive in the apocalypse that is swarming with Qs?"

"That's one hell of a question, but we really should be-"

"Come on… I got something to show you."

He vanished behind this opening between two panels of wall in the back of the store. I guess I was so startled at seeing this small man wearing a white lab coat in a Mattress Firm that I didn't even think about where he came from.

Samara pulled her cart off to the side and followed through the opening.

She was way more interested than me.

Between the panels was a stair set. It seemed to go down forever. It went so far that I couldn't see the bottom because the slanting roof was blocking my view.

I watched a movie called *Barbarian* before this world went to shit. I really don't like the idea of concrete catacombs after that; but here I was, walking down the world's longest stairway.

Eventually I made it to the bottom and found Samara and Desmond waiting on me in an elevator.

"We didn't think you were going to show," he said. He pushed a couple buttons when I got in the elevator, and we went down. "Powered by alien tech. Never runs out of power. Just like the lights you saw."

Truth be told, I didn't even wonder about how the lights were on.

When the elevator doors opened a giant empty tunnel was in front of us. I looked left to right, nothing but concrete on either side.

"Scary, huh?" Desmond asked. "Go left, you'll end up at an ocean, go right, you'll end up at an ocean."

He motioned us to follow him. He opened a door against a wall, and we entered a room filled with computers, tv screens, pictures taped to walls, and a small kitchen.

"Want a party pizza?" He asked.

He opened a freezer and pulled out one of those little square Totino's pizzas and threw it in the oven.

"Got a party here," he said, "need a party pizza."

The TVs were on and showing all sorts of things I never thought I'd see. On one a group of dog-like creatures slept in a cave, on another a city filled with mermaids was flourishing, another showed a man feeding a velociraptor and arguing with another man while he pointed to his shoes.

"What the fuck…" I said.

"Oh, those," Desmond said, "those are other dimensions. The aliens taught us how to do this so we could kind of keep up. If you mean the shoe argument; no clue, those guys are always arguing."

"Do you have a feed to where everyone went?"

"Earth-2?"

He clicked a few buttons on a keyboard and a screen displayed a city. A huge city. There were cars literally flying around and people just walking along like the three-foot-tall grey aliens walking by them weren't a big deal.

"That's why we're here," Desmond said, "Mattress Firm has been a nationwide coverup. We've been helping the aliens monitor other dimensions. They cut us a deal. Earth-2 was ours if we helped them fix some issues they created. Turns out it's partially their fault these goblins are here."

"What the fuck."

"Crazy, right? Well, the aliens were trying to do some weird dimension traveling and they blew it. Turns out they may be just as stupid as us. They didn't take into account that making the walls separating dimensions into Swiss cheese could make some things fall into the wrong places."

"What. The. Fuck."

"Yeah, sorta like putting the wrong kinds of fish together in a tank. Anyway, there's a whole military type force on Earth-2 that cleans the shit up."

"How?"

"How do I know? I'm on a year rotation here. Even though everyone left, there's a fifty-man skeleton crew across the US, we're all in state capitals, we just make sure nothing gets worse here."

"I…"

"Yeah, you're stuck. Are you like those rednecks I saw?"

"The Qs?"

"Yeah, the racists. They tried to kill me a few weeks ago. But I ran into a library. Dumb bastards must have been terrified of that place."

"Where…"

"Check this one out."

He flipped a few buttons, and a screen showed a small village made of trees. Sasquatch moved in and out of their homes. Samara walked over to the screen and touched it. She started shedding tears.

"It's his home," Desmond said standing beside me.

"Her," I said.

"Sorry, her home."

"How can we get there?"

"Well, the goblins messed up the portal in the Newport. It only goes to their home world now. But, if you go to their world, you can connect through another portal that will take you to this one…" he pointed to a screen showing humanoid frogs on beach. "Yeah, one of these guys came to Loveland. They opened a natural portal on their world, now they're experts. If you get there, they can get you to Samsquatch's home, and then from there they can get you to Earth-2. Kind of like a cryptid subway system."

Samara kept staring at the screen showing her home world and crying.

She finally noticed the frog people; her face distorted into pure rage.

"Oh yeah, I should mention, there's been some… tensions… between the frog folk and the bigfeet. Is bigfeet plural for bigfoot? I don't know."

"What kind of tension?"

"The frog folk accidentally created a portal that dropped the oldest and most revered of the Sasquatch into a world that is nothing but a vast ocean filled with predators. That's where Nessie came from. Y'all sure you don't want a pizza?"

We changed our minds and ate pizza. Desmond and I chatted about Earth before the goblins the whole time; Samara stared at the frog people.

"Pretty pissed still, huh, Samsquatch?" Desmond asked.

Samara grunted at the screen and clenched her fist.

This was going to be fun.

I asked Desmond what HIS plan to get out of here was.

He showed us some strange device that looked like a shower stall. It was basically a five-and-a-half-foot tall tube. Like a Pringle's can.

I asked why he couldn't just send us.

He said he could, maybe in a year when it turned on, but it would only take one of us, then the others would wait another year and it was the end of his shift coming up.

Capitalism lives.

When it's your day off, it's your day off goddamnit!

It didn't really matter; I didn't think Samara would fit. She was anxious about waiting however many months too, and so was I.

We'll just go the route that makes the least sense and go on this cryptid-dimension hopping subway.

Desmond escorted us up through the elevator again. He told us if we needed any help, just ask him.

We asked if he had any super-powered alien weaponry.

He said the greys are a peaceful species, mostly scientists.

I asked about the whole anal probing thing, because I'm a sixth grader.

He smirked and said everyone has their kinks.

"Stay safe, Desmond. Thank you," I told him as we shook hands.

"Keep an eye on Samsquatch," he said, "I'm gonna go boil some Pepsi."

With that he was gone and so were we.

We pushed our carts like two gossiping old women at a supermarket. Ok, so mainly me just ranting about how insane this all was.

Frogmen?

Aliens?

WHAT THE FUCK?

One of my bottles of deer piss exploded. I jerked back in a panic. Are ghosts here now too?

"Don't you fucking try it!" Yelled our old friend Gary while he pointed a rifle at Samara.

She growled.

"Take me there," he said.

"Where?" I asked, I genuinely didn't know what he meant.

"China. Are you really a fucking idiot? Mattress Firm. I saw y'all go in. I know they're keeping children down there for the Clintons."

"Yeah. Ok. Right this way."

I kept thinking Desmond had better have some sort of weapon.

I didn't know how to open the door, I just kept tapping at the spot it opened.

Samara shoved and it popped open.

Down the stairs, into the elevator, down we went.

"Have a drink, you racist fuck!" Desmond yelled as he splashed Gary with the contents of a boiling pot. Gary ran left down the corridor screaming at the top of his lungs. We stood there in silence listening for a couple minutes as his voice trailed away.

"What… the fuck."

"Y'all think I don't have a camera up top?"

"Makes sense. What was that? An alien chemical?"

"I told you I had to boil some Pepsi."

I picked up the gun Gary dropped and handed it to Desmond. He threw his arms up in a no way am I touching that motion.

"My ancestors were quakers."

"Sorry?"

"I don't know if you need to be. It's a quote from the Sandra Bullock movie *Ms. Congeniality*."

"Never seen it."

"It's the only damn DVD I've got down here."

We did the whole goodbye thing again. We took the rifle, maybe we could figure out how to use it. That idea was short lived when I accidentally shot a window out of a Wendy's when we were outside.

We put it in Samara's cart and went on our way.

We're in another hotel now. Tomorrow we're going to make a couple stops before we go up to the Newport.

We put it off today.

All I could think about was what happened last time, and I got cold feet.

Samara kept pointing to the bottles of deer piss like they were going to cheer me up.

They didn't.

They just reminded me about how fucking dumb I am that I forgot them the first time.

We did go outside though.

There is a used media store close to the hotel, so we went in and loaded up a few shopping carts they had—that looked stolen from a dollar store— with gaming systems, games, movies, anything we thought might help Desmond not watch *Miss Congeniality* every day.

He was hella appreciative, so much so that he gave us the DVD copy of *Miss Congeniality*.

Samara has watched it four times in a row.

I can't take it.

Sandra Bullock is hilarious in it, and I crack up every time Shatner is on screen. But I can't do this tomorrow night again.

Samara thinks every single gag is funny. She belly laughs and slaps the side of the bed at EVERY. SINGLE. THING.

She's also discovered Cheetos so that has been fun. Her side of the room is covered in empty Cheetos bags and Mountain Dew cans.

She's turned into a teenage boy.

She tried the flaming hot ones, that didn't go over so well. She let out a yell that hurt my gut and then offered me a can of Dewdie as an apology.

I accepted; I didn't want to hurt her feelings.

She's snoring now, ripping some crazy farts.

Real humdingers.

I'm going to try to tune it out and get rested for tomorrow.

Apparently, Cheetos and Mountain Dewdie a good diet for a Sasquatch does not make.

Poor Samara has been lying in bed holding her stomach and whining all day.

I don't think we're going anywhere.

I went and got some Pepto, she chugged fourteen bottles of it.

She's just been sleeping, ripping ass, and watching *Miss Congeniality.*

I went back to the store and found a copy of *The Legend of Boggy Creek*; that just seemed to upset her. When the people were scared of Bigfoot in the movie, she just looked so distant and sad. It was hard not to laugh at her, sitting there crying and having Cheetos farts.

She was ok with *Harry and the Hendersons*; that one made her laugh a few times.

She really, REALLY liked *Predator.*

We've been on a rotation of *Predator* followed by *Miss Congeniality* for the entire afternoon and evening.

She watches *Predator* completely cloaked.

I wonder what would happen if *Miss Congeniality* met the Predator?

Like, what if the Predator showed up at the beauty pageant?

My money is on Sandra Bullock.

Rowling thinks he's really fucking cute.

Let me explain how he isn't cute at all, but he's actually the ugliest, most mean-spirited little shit that ever walked the face of Earth.

Samara and I woke up today determined.

We covered ourselves in deer peepee, got our weapons, and headed out meaning so much business.

We walked in the front door of the Newport and nothing happened.

Right past the ticket booth and nothing happened.

Right up to where the goblins were sleeping last time, and nothing happened.

We looked at each other and squinted.

The deer pee could NOT be working THIS good, is what I was thinking.

Samara went to the portal and waved her hand over the control panel.

When it turned on it didn't really make a sound. It sounded like someone flipped a vacuum cleaner on and then shut it off.

The portal itself looked like purple water. It wasn't deep but it rippled like the ocean on a stormy night.

We looked at each other and shrugged.

When we got right to the portal Rowling landed in front of us and puked.

The deer piss worked in a trap at least.

We heard the thud of other goblins landing around us. They must have been waiting in the rafters.

They all puked.

Every single one of them.

I turned to swing a baseball bat at Rowling and slipped in the puke.

The puke didn't cushion the blow I took to the head at all.

When I was fading out of vision, I saw Samara being fought to the ground by a hoard of the little green fuckers.

I woke up when my notebook hit me in the face, just like in the Q prison. Only this time it was a storage closet and Rowling was flipping me off after throwing the notebook.

He set us up.

We fell for it.

Now there's a portal open for them.

We were in the storage closet all morning until one of the little shits got a little too arrogant. It opened the door and came in with a cattle prod. I have no idea where it got it from. I didn't have time to ask because as soon as it steered it out toward me Samara grabbed it and used it to pull the unsuspecting goblin to her.

She just kept stomping on its body because it was apparently the spider ruining her morning shower.

The room was covered in greens, blues, and purples from the thing's blood. The door was open.

Samara let out an annoyed grunt after she stepped out. The next motion was her punching the wall. When I came through there was a multicolored splat and a hole in the wall where a goblin used to stand.

She was fucking mad.

I'm talking MAD mad.

We didn't encounter anything else until we reached the stage area. There were hundreds of the fuckers there.

They all turned to look at us while they stood around the portal.

They somehow managed to get the thing on the ground and it looked like a massive purple swimming pool.

I looked around and didn't see Rowling anywhere, so I assumed he had already gone through.

The sound of metal being ripped from metal made me look up in time to see Samara ripping apart chunks of rafters.

Can she fucking fly now???

A whole section of metal fell straight down from at least one hundred feet and mashed a ton of goblins.

It looked like someone dropped a ton of paint on the floor and covered all the ugly fucks.

She dropped down on top of the rafter and started grabbing the things and either throwing them against walls or ripping them apart.

Samara was done playing games.

I got tackled off the stage by one of the things. It landed on my chest, and I grabbed its arms to stop it from killing me with its razor blade talons. We were staring into each other's eyes and screaming out for more strength. The goblin's head fell beside my head, and I was covered in blue and purple.

Samara picked me up with the hand that wasn't holding the severed arm of a goblin and threw me into the portal.

As soon as I saw the purple meeting my face, I came out of the other side like I was doing a dive.

I landed on cold, hard, compacted dirt and slid.

Shortly after me, Samara flew out and landed on her ass.

She jumped up and ripped a ton of wires from the makeshift portal device the goblins had used to highjack the Earth to Earth-2 pipeline.

We were in what appeared to be an empty room.

It was a large dome shape made up of a weird foamy material that was shaped like tree branches. When I touched one it made my skin itchy. It felt like touching insulation but had the same texture as wet clay.

Samara did not give a fuck.

She charged through one of the walls. On the other side five goblins were staring at us while they ate what appeared to be the side of a building.

They must be using the portal as a way to bring food from off world.

We could have potentially starved all of them when we destroyed the portal.

I really don't care.

There was one goblin that was the size of a kitten; it was being held by a full grown one.

Adorable.

I flipped it off.

The one holding it looked at Samara; it just stood up and walked away. Not even in a hurry. Just like it realized it forgot its food in the oven or something.

We were in some sort of cave system, only the caves were made of the same shit as the dome. Out here it was all bright purple though.

Samara marched forward and stomped right through their noon time concrete feast.

I followed her because she meant business.

We made a few turns before we were outside and staring at two green suns in a pink sky.

I had to pause and say "whoa" because I'm a human.

Samara isn't, so she kept going right across this blue empty ground.

It felt like the surface of a trampoline, so I tried it.

I did bounce a little, but not like I would have if it truly were a trampoline.

There were entrances into other cave systems all around us, goblins stood inside the doorways and shrieked at us.

One of them threw a heavy piece of something that was yellow in color. I didn't get to examine it because as soon as it went in the air close to Samara, she snatched it and threw it back.

It hit the goblin hard in the shoulder causing it to fall and make this agonizing sound.

She walked into one of the caverns like she knew exactly where she was going. She sniffed the air twice and kept going.

We were in another dome, this one had three goblins messing with wires on a portal unit.

One marched toward us shrieking something that sounded a whole lot like their version of "who the fuck are you? You can't be here!" But it was cut short by Samara backhanding it and sending it flying into a wall.

The others just stepped aside.

Samara walked through the portal like we hadn't just traipsed through the goblin home world unharmed.

I paused at the entrance and said, "so sorry about all of this. She's just a little pissed. Anyway, eat shit."

That was when I took two steps forward and got lifted off the ground by an eight-foot-tall frog standing on two legs.

Guess where I'm writing this?

Guess.

Another cell.

Samara's favorite part in *Predator* is when Arnold gets all ready to fight and there's that musical montage of both preparing to kill the other. That, but at the end, where Arnold puts on the mud face paint and screams at the sky; Samara loves that shit.

Here's a long story to explain how I found out.

First things first, I'm about dogshit tired of waking up in places I can't just leave when I'm ready to leave. Frog land was no different.

This time it was a bamboo type branch tied together by vine.

Their world looked like a massive swamp.

Shallow water, trees, foliage. You know what it looks like. The water was all perfectly clear for the most part, some areas were a little foggy but mostly you could see the narrow paths you were walking on.

I noticed very quickly if you took a wrong step, you'd be in water that looked to be bottomless.

Judging by some of the creatures swimming in those depths—and the frog like bones at the bottom— I may not even notice I fell in before being munched on.

The creatures swam like dolphins but had serpentine-like bodies. Fins lined both sides all the way up to the head of what looked like an ant. Picture an aquatic centipede, that's as close to what this thing was as I could describe.

Other smaller insect like fish swam in the shallows. Bees with fins instead of wings, flies with tentacles, I even saw a dragonfly the size of a Great White Shark.

The frogs would splash their tongues down into the water and come up with some of the surface insects; the nastiest crunching you could hear would then start.

They put us in our little cages; we at least had a hammock made of vines to let us sleep without the fear of drowning.

When the sun was rising, which was just a normal sun oddly enough, a group of four frog people with weird silver guns showed up and took us from our cells. They were friendly to me but not Samara. One of them shoved her forward and the other stuck out its foot sending her splashing face first in the shallow water. She jumped up and grabbed one by its neck. They made clicking noises and spoke some words that sounded like English but distorted by their mouth structure. She let go and complied.

Frogman must be her second language.

We were escorted to a building that looked to have been built on Earth but collapsed in transportation. It was just a one-story building, but all the walls were falling inward.

We went in a front door and before us was a human man sitting up in a bed. He looked ancient. Above his head someone had painted the words "the last man."

"You've caused quite a stir here, young man," said the old man, "they believe you helped this being open a portal to unleash a monster upon us."

"Samara is cool," I said, "these two are the ones who shoved her over."

"I suppose you know of the Great War?"

"Thanks for ignoring me. Yeah, these assholes opened a portal under Samara's people's oldest living member."

"A mistake. The tech was so young then."

"They could have apologized."

"Ah, yes, I suppose so. But you know how humanity refuses to accept when they're wrong."

"These are frog people, guy."

"Global warming happened. Scientists found a way to make humans amphibious, as well as other species, in one generation-"

"Gonna stop you there because that's not a story I feel like jamming about right now. We need to get to Samara's world."

"They'll help you with that. But you need to help them with a problem you caused first."

Two new frog people carried the body of another and laid it on the ground before us. The body was covered in deep lacerations.

Rowling.

"The little shit…" I said.

"So, you do know it?"

"Yeah, it's a real piece of shit too."

"It killed this man. One of their highest-ranking minds. Then ran off into nature. Then you came not an hour later."

"I see…"

"You see how they may think it's your fault."

"I said I see."

"Not so blind then, eh?"

"No. No I'm not."

We stood there awkwardly for at least a minute. I think he lost track of where his speech was going.

Samara had it figured anyway, she tapped the body, made a stance mimicking Rowling, then pointed to me and herself, then made a motion of cutting her own throat.

The frogs grunted, Samara nodded at one of them, and we were then walking through knee deep water hunting the little bastard.

They gave me one of the guns; a small tutorial showed me I just hit a switch and a red dot appeared, then when I pressed a button, a green ray shot out. Whatever the ray hit cooked up like one of Desmond's party pizzas and looked dehydrated AF.

We marched through swampland, following all the clues Rowling had left behind.

Not subtle either; we're talking trees with massive chunks cut out of them. He must have been using his claws to grip the trees as he jumped.

A giant ladybug crashed through our path at one point, it had flippers and they splashed through the shallows.

I was hoping we could go home before we ran into whatever massive version of a stink bug was here because I was not in the mood.

We found Rowling in another caved-in building. He was punching a teleportation device and trying to get it to take him back home I assume. He must have known about the feud with the Sasquatch and Frogmen and hoped he could lead us here to get rid of us.

His head jerked in our direction immediately.

Why? You ask.

Because Samara painted her face with mud and stood up screaming like Arnold before charging in his direction.

The frogs were pissed.

They dove into the deeper water and swam so fast I could have used them to tow me for skiing.

Rowling got the portal to work and dove through before anyone reached him.

By the time I made it over the frog people were shrieking and pointing at Samara, and she had already punched one out.

I stepped between them and pointed to the portal. I put Samara's hand on the back of my shirt and hoped she got the message to hold on.

When I stuck my head through, I saw Rowling swimming through a massive pool, maybe an aquarium. Beyond him was a serpent-like neck connected to a head filled with teeth.

Plesiosaur.

A dinosaur in an aquarium.

I watched as Rowling barely got out of the water before becoming din din.

He saw me looking, flipped me off, and slashed his claws through a control panel.

The water in the aquarium started to swirl like it was going down a drain.

Rowley ran away into the depths of whatever world and building he had found.

I was thrown back hard and landed in the deep water. I opened my eyes and saw a wasp swimming at me with a tentacle emerging from where the stinger should have been.

Samara pulled me from the water while arguing with the Frogmen.

The Frogmen took my gun and left us in the wreckage of the building.

That's how I found out what Samara's favorite scene in *Predator* is.

Samara was messing with the portal all night.

She would hit a few buttons, stick her head through, come back.

One time she came back with a cactus latched onto her head. It was like some weird spider thing. She held it up in the air like she was going to smash it, but then lightly tossed it back in. She looked at me and shrugged.

I asked her what we should do about Rowling, she shrugged.

I guess that's good enough for me. He's someone else's problem now.

At some point I fell asleep; when I woke up there was a face staring at me that was a Sasquatch but was not Samara.

I sat up in a panic to find I was in a dome built from tree branches.

Samara sat on a large rock beside the male I saw in her vision. The one who was staring at me was just slightly shorter than me.

It hugged me as soon as I stood up, I hugged it back.

The male stood up and outstretched his hand to me. When I took it, I felt a deep sense of gratitude fill my body.

He was thanking me for helping Samara get back here.

I said, "thanks, little guy… er… girl," when the child let go of my waist. I had no idea whether it was a boy or girl.

Samara pointed to herself and shook her head no, then to the male and shook her head yes.

I don't need Meghan Trainor pooping next to a spy kid to figure that out anymore.

We went outside to about fifty other Sasquatch; no joke, there were so many.

They were all cheering for me and hugging me.

Society may not believe in Sasquatch, but they believed in me today.

Horrible joke.

Samara took me to a group of Sasquatch working on a portal device. They were trying to get it to a specific point.

She pointed at me, the portal, and then the ground.

They're trying to get it to take me home.

I smiled and said, "thanks."

The rest of the day was spent eating and playing games with the children.

The food was fish every time, but each time tasted completely different. Some were fried, some were baked; I have no idea how they did either.

The little ones kept making me throw rocks into an empty field and then laughing their hairy asses off when I didn't throw it even a fraction as far as they could.

It's all been a bit overwhelming.

When night fell, we went back to the dome and drank some beverage that tasted like a mix between tea and vanilla.

"Way better than Mountain Dewdie, right?" I asked.

Samara laughed, the other two looked confused.

An inside joke between Bigfoot and Jim.

I'm looking forward to tomorrow.

Even if they can't get me home for a while, I feel welcome here.

I'm not worried about anything killing me, starving, or loneliness.

I'll see what tomorrow brings, but this is the best I've felt in a long time.

I'm leaving this notebook behind.

I'm done writing after this entry.

Samara woke me up today as happy as can be. Her son hugged me, her partner did the same.

The portal was working.

One Sasquatch stood beside it making it work and looking very dignified. I can't explain it, but he looked downright fancy.

Samara nodded at the portal and then pulled her son and partner in close.

"Go ahead, go to your people," is what her actions were telling me.

"Thank you," I said, "thank you for being a friend, a savior, and for opening those Spaghetti-Os for me. I'll bring Claire to visit."

Samara nodded and a tear slid down her face.

She picked me up and hugged me like I was a small stuffed toy.

When she sat me down, I decided this awkward moment could go on forever if we let it, so I walked to the portal. I took a deep breath, turned to wave goodbye to my newest friend, and stepped through.

A guy in a lab coat jumped back when I stepped into his small room.

"Holy shit," he said, "where did YOU come from?"

"I'm Jim Tiptree. I was left behind on Earth."

"You're not related to Claire Tiptree, are you?"

"We're married."

"I know. I just wanted to have one of those Marvel movie moments where I asked that, and you nodded then the scene cut to her fighting dinosaurs."

"I love those parts."

"Me too."

"Wait… dinosaurs?"

He pointed to a screen that showed Claire surrounded by a pile of dead giant lizards. She was covered in blood and spinning in a circle giving each one the bird.

Claire…

"Where is that?" I asked.

"It's where her mission took her. After you got left behind, she signed up to fix all of these dimensional bleeds."

"What?"

"Well, when the goblins-"

"Desmond told me."

"Oh… speaking of. We lost contact with the West Virginia operator on Earth. We sent Desmond to check. The guy was dead. Someone drove one of the golf carts all the way from Columbus to Charleston and killed the poor guy. They painted "#wwg1wga" on a wall and fled through the portal."

"Where did he go?"

"Same place Claire is going next actually."

"Where? And can you get me there?"

"She's going to a place we call 'Grave.' It's a dimension like Earth where an alien spore turned the dead into mindless husks that kill and eat the living. Some of the living got possessed and became… well… vampires."

"Vampire dimension. Get me there."

Tomorrow I'm going to this other place to meet up with Claire. I just hope the fuckers don't sparkle.

I can be hella long winded with this section, so I'm gonna make a real honest effort to not do that. K... here we go.

To Breanna, I started writing this book as a way to talk about cryptids; she has to hear me ramble on and on and on about them, so I thought I'd give her a little break. Thanks as always for being the best wife of all time and putting up with all of the nonsense.

To Mercedes Mone/Varnado. Thank you for being my hero and inspiring me to always be the weirdo I want to be; and to work towards it as passionately as I possibly can.

To Kyra R. Torres, Thanks for being my ~*BFF*~, cohost, publishing partner, and co-writer on all things Hot Pink Satanism. You rule ass even if you think you don't, and I wouldn't trade our convos about the stupidest shit for anything. The world truly isn't ready for a gay Mexican chicken sandwich.

To Sarah Jane Huntington, Thanks for being so authentically you. Your drive and attitude is a huge inspiration to me, and I hope one day we get proof of aliens and not just more Oreos.

CJ Sampera, my one and only FEIE D, you're my favorite juggalo, one of the only reasons I didn't quit writing, and I love you so much, boo boo.

Caitlin Marceau, Kryptkeeper Kyle may despise you, but I think you're hella cool.

Adam Hulse, your photoshop skills are shite, but you're alright.

Wendy Dalrymple, you the realest.

Brian Berry, quit tagging me in pickle shit and make me a cheesecake.

Eric, Nikki, Nora, and Sonny Pierce, I wouldn't watch wrestling with anyone else. Thanks for making me fall in love with professional speedo fighting again.

Crystal Cottrill, thanks for always supporting me and listening to my stupid ass story ideas.

Cody Lambert, I wish you were as cool as Jeremiah.

Jeremiah Cullen, I like you better than Cody.

Jake, Josh, and Bridget Kennedy, thanks for being day one and not killing me.

Jesse Mowery, please don't male me go to any Christmas themed haunted houses.

Christopher McCormick, you my ghost boo and I can't wait to hang out in person at cons.

Dawn Shea @ D&T Publishing, thanks for adopting Kyra and I; we promise to always be your weird kids.

Andrew Robert @ Darklit Press, thanks for always having my back, and taking me on as the dickhead who put a dick-dragon in your pirate series.

Emily Gibson Cardwell, you rule ass.

Ola Allison, you also rule ass.

Missy Kritzer, yet another ruler of ass.

Casey Smallwood, more ass ruling.

Here's a list of indie authors that I love dearly, and you should to:

Kyra R. Torres, Sarah Jane Huntington, CJ Sampera, Adam Hulse, Caitlin Marceau, Brian Berry, Wendy Dalrymple, Alysson Hasson, M.E. Grey, Jeremy Megargee, Bridget Nelson, Jeff Strand, Derek Hutchins, Catherine McCarthy, BENTOOLAZYTOREMOVEHISHALLOWEENNAME I DONT KNOW YOUR NAME BEN, H. Everend, Alexander Mercant, Remo Maccartney, Christopher Robertson, Garth Jones, R.K. Latch.

If I forgot you put your name here___________________

ABOUT DAMIEN CASEY

Damien Casey hates writing these things because when he was created in a lab the scientists kept making him talk about his past all the time.

Kind of like *The Fly 2*

Actually, Damien Casey is Jeff Goldblum.

ALSO BY DAMIEN CASEY

Hot Pink Satanism (w/ Kyra R Torres)

Chocolate pudding mixed with cotton candy and molded into an inverted cross, Hot Pink Satanism is a Horror-Rom-Com for the evilest of lil' cuties.

From D&T Publishing

Coffin Dodger

When your favorite actors aren't acting, they're dealing with ghost-snakes, giant crocodiles, spiders with human faces, and cults kidnapping them. One of these cults kidnaps a group of actors from a cult classic horror series. This cult forces the group to play a game where they have to face their biggest fears in order to gain eternal life. They don't even want eternal life. It's all pretty inconvenient.

The Village of Gill

Four friends travel to a remote island where something... fishy is going on.
A horror/comedy choose your own adventure story for fans of creature features from the 80's.

<u>In the Palm of the Left Hand Black</u>

Cover and interior artwork by Christopher McCormick.

Frist!

Five Years (That's All We've Got)

Smoking Section

Pretty Penny the Pissed-Off Poltergeist Vs. The Q'Anon Army

Holy Diver

COMING SOON FROM DAMIEN CASEY

The Nine Teeth of the River Styx

A crew of pirates meet Lilith and search through the nine levels of Hell for Satan's treasure. They face monstrosities of mutilated flesh, elephantine insects, and a possessed parrot.

Coming October from Darklit Press as part of the Darklit Sails series of "Pirate Horror" novels and novellas

HEY KIDS!
CRYPTOTEEOLOGY
GET THESE SHIRTS WITH MONEY!
DOZENS OF CRYPTIDS & MONSTERS NEED YOUR MONEY SUPPORT
Help me support them by purchasing a soft, comfy, cozy Cryptoteeology t-shirt with your favorite cryptid or monster printed on it.
You absolutely, positively, probably, most definitely maybe, may or may not regret your decision but you might feel all warm and fuzzy that you helped me help them.
DISCLAIMER: None of the money from these sales go to any cryptids or monsters. It all goes to me, myself and I because that's just how capitalism works.
ADULT X-SMALL THROUGH 5XL
BUY MY STUFF!
HERE'S A COUPON FOR NOTHING
SAVE 0%
OFF OF EVERY PURCHASE!
DON'T CUT OUT THIS COUPON!!!
WHAT KIND OF IDIOT CAME UP WITH THE IDEA OF PUTTING COUPONS IN BOOKS AND COMIC BOOKS IN THE FIRST PLACE?
WWW.CRYPTOTEEOLOGY.COM
LIKE AND FOLLOW US ON FACEBOOK AND INSTAGRAM

Twitter- @3bpublishing
Instagram- @3bpublishing
www.3-bpublishing.com